LiTTLE PASSPORTS®

Knights and Falcons

Written by Megan E. Bryant

Illustrated by Carrie English

First paperback edition printed in 2022 by Little Passports, Inc.
Copyright © 2022 Little Passports
All rights reserved
Cover illustration by Rhiannon Davenport
Manufactured in China
10 9 8 7 6 5 4 3 2

Little Passports, Inc.
121 Varick Street, Floor 3, New York, NY 10013
www.littlepassports.com
ISBN: 978-1-953148-14-8

Contents

1 To the Faire! 1

2 The Warning Light 14

3 The Tower of London 20

4 The Woman in White 25

5 Birds of Prey 36

6 Any Volunteers? 40

7 A Difficult Decision 57

8 Tintagel 63

9 Center Stage 71

10 Battery Critical 87

11 A Hard Reset 91

12 Past and Present 96

1

To the Faire!

Sam's feet stomped on the sidewalk as he ran to Compass Community Center. It was a big day—the traveling Olde English Faire had arrived!

Sam, his best friend Sofia, and their families

had been planning for weeks. Visitors to the Faire would experience what it was like to live in medieval England between the years 500 and 1500. Sofia's mother, Mama Lyla, had even hired historical reenactors to give the Faire an extra level of authenticity!

For Sam, the best part of the Faire was that he was going to play a role in it! And now that the reenactors had arrived, Sam would find out what his part would be.

With a few more strides, Sam crossed the entrance to the event.

The reenactors were already hard at work erecting colorful tents, wooden stalls, and booths. A cart pulled by a donkey turned abruptly, right in front of Sam.

Sam skidded to a stop. "Whoa! Sorry!" he said, catching his breath.

The donkey brayed, and its owner laughed. "Our apologies to you, young master," she said with a flourish of her hand. "Bertram here is excited for the festivities."

She patted Bertram's neck and guided him on.

Another woman passed by, carrying heavy bolts of fabric in her arms. "Pardon! Pardon! Coming through!" she cried. This time, Sam got out of the way even quicker!

The event space was a sea of faces, but none was the face Sam was searching for. He knew Sofia was just as eager to learn her role in the Faire as he was. She had to be around here somewhere.

Just as he was about to ask someone if they'd seen her, a voice called from behind.

"Sam! Sam!" Sofia yelled. "They did it! They posted the list!"

"Already?" Sam asked, turning to meet her. "Did you check it?"

"Not yet," Sofia said. "I was looking for you."

"Let's go!" Sam said.

"*Vamos!*" Sofia replied.

Together, they ran over to a long scroll of parchment tacked to a nearby wall. Sam scanned it for his name while Sofia scanned it for hers. Sam ran his finger down the names.

Ellie: Farmer
Mani: Astronomer
Max: Carpenter
Mia: Doctor
Mikey: Clockmaker
Ruby: Blacksmith
Sam: Knight
Sofia: Falconer
Scout: Singing Bard
Toby: Court Jester

Falconer sounded like a great role for bird-adoring Sofia. But Sam . . . a knight? He took a step back and tilted his head, still staring at the list. Next to him, Sofia hopped with glee.

"A falconer!" she cried. "Perfect!"

"Congratulations!" Sam said. "What exactly does a falconer do, though?"

Sofia paused mid-hop. "That's a good question," she said. "They must care for the falcons and train them maybe?"

Sam could already see it in his mind: Sofia, the falconer! He wished he felt as confident about his role.

"And you," Sofia said, still bubbling with excitement, "a brave, bold, daring knight!"

Sam tried to muster another smile.

"What's wrong?" Sofia asked.

"Weren't knights ferocious warriors?" Sam asked. "Didn't they wear armor and fight battles? That doesn't sound like me."

"But that wasn't all they did, right?" Sofia said. Then her eyes brightened. "Let's ask Mama!"

"Great idea," Sam said. Maybe Mama Lyla would help put him in the medieval spirit.

Sam and Sofia wove their way through the courtyard, which was getting busier every minute. In the center of the courtyard, Sofia's dad, Papai Luiz, was overseeing the construction of a royal box at the jousting arena. Billowing canopies swooped against a brilliant blue sky. There were more animals nearby—clucking chickens and some playful goats frolicking in their pen.

Sofia paused to watch a woman kneel near the chickens, holding out her hand with her fingers pinched together. As if by magic, the chickens started moving toward her!

"How did she do that?" Sofia gawked in amazement.

The woman looked over and smiled at Sam and Sofia. "They know I've got a pocket full of grain for them," she said, patting her apron. "Now they come whether or not it's feeding time!"

"Neat trick," Sofia said to Sam as they continued on their way.

"Look," Sam said. "I see your dad!"

"*Olá*, Papai!" Sofia called. "We're looking for Mama. You know where she is?"

Papai rubbed his chin. "Hmm. I think she was setting up the outdoor kitchen," he replied. "I'll text her to find out for sure."

Papai reached into his pocket for his phone and tapped on the screen. Then he tapped again. He tapped one more time, then frowned. "Frozen," he said with a sigh.

"Is it broken?" Sofia asked.

"No, I don't think so," he said. "It just needs a hard reset." He pressed some buttons on the side of the phone, holding them down until the screen went black. "In a few minutes, it should restart, good as new."

"We'll keep looking for Mama," Sofia said. "Good luck with your phone, Papai!"

As they turned to continue their search, Sofia paused and sniffed at the air. "You smell that?"

Sam sniffed. "It smells delicious!"

"Follow that scent!" Sofia declared.

The aroma led Sam and Sofia straight to Mama Lyla. She was tending a large black cauldron over a crackling fire, wearing an apron made of coarse fabric. With a wooden spoon in her hand, she waved to Sam and Sofia.

"Welcome, young travelers, to the Faire—and the feast!" She spoke deeply in a funny voice. "Come rest a spell and sup with us!" She lifted a gloppy spoonful from the pot. "It's almost ready."

"I don't have much of an appetite," Sam said.

"Well, I'd like to eat it, ready or not!" a new voice said.

Sam and Sofia turned around as a man wearing a long brown robe approached. A big bushy beard covered much of his face.

"Of course you would, Brother Andrew," Mama Lyla said warmly as she sliced a thick piece of bread for the visitor.

"Is this your brother?" Sam asked.

Mama Lyla laughed. "Brother Andrew is his character," she explained. "He's playing a friar. "

"What a cool job," Sofia said. She took a big bite of her own bread slice.

"Ever since my first Faire, when I was a lad just about your age, I've been hooked," Brother Andrew said. "Perchance you will be too. Tell us, now, what will your role be?"

"I'll be a falconer," Sofia said. "And Sam will be a knight!"

"Oh-ho!" Brother Andrew chortled. "Excellent additions to the Faire. Falconry, yes, not just a pastime of kings and queens but an essential skill for putting food on the table. Thank you, m'lady." He accepted the bread from Mama Lyla and turned to Sam. "And a knight! Brave, daring, and gallant, I'm sure."

Brother Andrew thumped Sam on the back so hard, Sam almost fell over. He marveled at Brother Andrew. It truly seemed like he'd traveled through time to join them in the present day.

"How do you do it?" Sam asked. "How do you make sure that you play your role correctly?"

"Being true to the historical record is important," Brother Andrew explained. "If we stray too far from what we know to be factual, it's not as authentic an experience." He glanced over at Mama Lyla. "None of us want that."

"Well said," Mama Lyla remarked. "It's all about research, research, research. And sometimes that means going straight to the source."

The words hung in the air even after Mama Lyla went to inspect the construction of a nearby booth; even after Brother Andrew used a dagger to hack off another hunk of bread; even after the flock of chickens passed by again, delighting Sofia with their clucks.

Maybe going "straight to the source" was exactly what Sam needed to do. And he'd of course have to bring Sofia.

Sam and Sofia weren't just best friends. They were also adventurers who shared a big secret. Not so long ago, Sam's aunt Charlie had showed them a new invention in her lab: a cherry-red scooter she'd designed and built using advanced technology. The scooter was no ordinary vehicle. The scooter could transport Sam and

Sofia anywhere in the world in a flash.

Sam turned to Sofia. "I wonder," he began.

Sofia's eyes instantly brightened. "Go on . . ."

"I wonder if we need to go *straight to the source*," Sam said in a low voice. "To England!"

"Of course!" Sofia exclaimed. "You can learn more about knights."

"And you can find out all about falconers," Sam finished.

As more reenactors continued to arrive, the best friends slipped away from the bustle of the courtyard without being noticed.

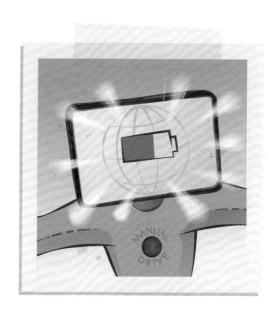

2

The Warning Light

Sam and Sofia ran to the house Sam shared with his aunt Charlie. Once there, they entered the garage, which was home to Aunt Charlie's lab. It was cool and quiet inside, with a special feeling hanging in the air. There was a certain sensation—of anticipation, of excitement—that always seemed present here. It was one of Sam's favorite places in the world.

"Quick scooter check, and we'll be off!" Sofia announced as she yanked the tarp off the red scooter. It was sitting quietly in the corner, glimmering faintly, almost as if it had been waiting for them.

Sofia peeked into the compartment under the seat. "Snacks, water bottles, sweatshirts—check, check, and check," she reported. Then she snapped the seat closed again. "And I have my notebook, of course."

"Of course," Sam replied with a grin. Sofia never left home without her special notebook, just like Sam never left home without his camera. Sofia's notebook was filled with doodles, thoughts, and lists, like the ongoing list of every bird she'd ever seen.

Sam climbed aboard the scooter and powered

up the touchscreen. A familiar image of a spinning globe appeared.

HELLO EXPLORERS!

Where would you like to travel?

"Okay," Sam said. "First, some research."

His fingers slid across the touchscreen as he entered his question. "Where can I learn more about life in medieval England?" he asked the screen as he typed.

The computer was quick to respond.

"England is full of sites of historical significance from the country's storied past," Sam read aloud. Sofia whipped out her notebook as Sam continued. "The Tower of London, near the banks of the River Thames, was constructed during the medieval period. It is now a time capsule in England's capital city, both a tourist destination and a fortress where the Crown Jewels are still securely stored."

"Well, we have to go there!" Sofia said.

"This sounds good too!" Sam said. He read on. "Fans of King Arthur and the Knights of the Round Table would also be well suited to visit Tintagel, the site of King Arthur's Great Halls."

"Tintagel." Sofia made a note. "Got it!"

Sam moved aside as Sofia typed another question. "Where do falconers—"

Sofia's words stopped abruptly.

"What's wrong?" Sam asked.

When Sofia pointed at the corner of the screen, a slow sinking feeling settled into Sam's stomach. The battery symbol wasn't at 100% like usual. Sam tapped on the symbol. The battery, usually fully charged, was at 70%.

Sofia leaned over, peering down at the outlet

on the wall. "It's not plugged in," she said.

The friends looked at each other. They both knew it was risky to set off on an adventure without a fully charged battery.

"Well," Sam said, "we'll just have to make the best of it. And be fast—even faster than usual."

Where to Visit:

Tower of London

Tintagel - King Arthur's Great Halls

Keep an eye on the battery!

"I'll keep an extra-close watch on the battery," Sofia promised, writing a reminder in her notebook. "If we leave England when the scooter has at least 15 percent battery, we should be able to make it home."

Sam nodded. He didn't want to think about the alternative. On all their adventures, they'd never once found themselves stranded in another country.

"Let's start with the Tower of London," Sam decided. "Maybe we'll see the Crown Jewels!"

Once more, Sam's fingers skittered across the touchscreen as he typed their destination.

He took a deep breath and held on tight as a blindingly bright light enveloped the red scooter, and Sam and Sofia along with it.

Whiz . . . Zoom . . . FOOP!

3

The Tower of London

By now, Sam knew exactly what to expect when the scooter whooshed him around the world: the hollow whistling sound in his ears; the countless sparkling lights that surrounded the scooter like a protective orb. No matter how many times Sam took this wild ride to a new country, though, he never got tired of it, and his heart never stopped pounding with excitement about what might happen next.

As the twinkling sparkles began to fade, Sam loosened his grip on the handlebars and blinked his eyes—once, twice, three times—until he could see clearly. He and Sofia had left Aunt Charlie's lab and Compass Court far behind.

The sky overhead was a mottled gray as clouds scudded across it. For a moment, Sam wondered if the air felt damp because it had just rained or because the rain was about to begin.

A nearby street was crowded with traffic, including sleek black cabs and tall double-decker buses, red just like the scooter.

"Sam," Sofia said, pointing. "I think that's it. The Tower of London!"

Sam raised his camera to his face.

Click-click!

Right there, in the midst of all the hustle and bustle of the city, was an ancient-looking fortress. Gray- and cream-colored stones formed tall, imposing walls, while arched windows stared out from the structure like eyes. And there wasn't just one tower but several, each capped with a domed top.

The Tower of London wasn't nearly as tall as the skyscrapers nearby, but the air of mystery surrounding it made it feel just as impressive. Sam couldn't wait to go inside. But first . . .

"Where should we hide the scooter?" he asked.

Sofia peered around and pointed at a wide

river nearby. "That must be the Thames," she said. "Maybe there's a spot along the water where we can tuck it away."

Sam and Sofia explored the outer grounds until they found a shaded spot along the river, away from most visitors. It was just the right size for safely storing the scooter.

"And now, the Tower awaits!" Sofia announced.

The massive iron gates were open wide, but that didn't make them feel any less imposing. Inside the thick walls surrounding the fortress was a wide, grassy lawn. It was like the Tower had its own park.

"Look!" Sofia said, noticing a cluster of jet-black birds across the grass.

"Are they crows?" Sam asked.

"I'd have to get a little closer to know for sure," Sofia replied, then her eyes lit up. "I have an idea," she said.

She walked slowly across the green grass

until she was a few feet from the birds. Then Sofia knelt down, holding out her hand with her fingers pinched together, just like the woman at the Faire had done for the chickens. Sam could hardly believe his eyes when one of the birds cocked its head and began to strut toward her!

"Sofia!" he whispered in excitement. "It's coming closer! You're doing it!"

"And you'd better stop right away!" a new voice said sternly.

4

The Woman in White

Sam and Sofia spun around. They saw a boy about their age standing behind them, his face furrowed into a frown.

"I'm sorry!" Sofia said quickly. "What—what was I doing wrong?"

"You're not supposed to feed the ravens," he said importantly. "It's not good for them."

Sam and Sofia exchanged a glance. "Ravens! Of course," Sofia said. "Don't worry. My hand is empty. I just wanted to get a better look. I love birds. I'd never want to hurt them."

The boy's face melted into a smile at once. "Apologies," he said. "The way you were crouched over, I thought you had a handful of crisps or something. The Tower ravens are famous, you know." He looked at them like a proud parent. "I'm always trying to look out for them, just like my uncle. My name is Nicholas."

Sam and Sofia quickly introduced themselves. "What makes the ravens famous?" Sam asked.

"According to legend," Nicholas said, his voice

dropping low dramatically, "the Tower has always been guarded by six ravens. The stories say that if the ravens ever leave, the Tower, and England, will fall."

Sofia whistled, impressed. "That's a lot of pressure for a bird," she said.

Nicholas smiled. "We take our legends pretty seriously," he said. "My uncle—he's the Ravenmaster—"

"What?" Sofia exclaimed. "That's his job?"

"Sort of," Nicholas said. "Uncle Richard is a guard here—a Yeoman Warder—and because he knows so much about birds, he's the Ravenmaster too. It's all part of his official duties. He's shown me how smart the ravens are. They can play games and solve puzzles. But be careful, because ravens can be quite fierce too."

Sofia scribbled away in her notebook.

"Sounds like you know a lot about the Tower of London," Sam said.

Nicholas looked down, but his smile gave away how pleased he was by the compliment. "A fair bit," he replied. "I do like to come here on the weekends to visit my uncle. He lives here, you know. I'm lucky I've never seen one of the ghosts, but that's probably because I always leave when the Tower is locked for the night."

"Ghosts?" Sam and Sofia said at the same time.

"Oh yes, the Tower is right famous for its ghosts," Nicholas told them. "Some say that Anne Boleyn, one of King Henry VIII's wives, still walks the very same grounds she roamed when she was alive."

Sam nervously fidgeted with the camera strap hanging around his neck.

"Spooky," Sofia said with a shiver.

"And that's just the start," Nicholas continued. "There used to be a zoo here, and some say ghost animals can be heard and even seen when the conditions are right. In particular, a ferocious ghost bear has frightened guards half to death!"

Sam gulped. "R-really?" he asked. His voice came out more quivery than he meant it to. *A knight shouldn't be scared of ghosts*, he thought. *Even the kind with huge paws and sharp teeth.* He shivered.

"I mean, I've never seen the ghost bear," Nicholas said. Then he puffed out his chest. "But I keep trying! And then, of course, there's the Woman in White."

"What's she famous for?" Sofia asked.

Sam sort of wished that they could change the subject, but was curious at the same time.

Nicholas leaned forward as he lowered his voice. "A ghostly woman in white robes, who appears when you least expect it," he whispered. "She's famous for . . ."

"What?" Sofia cried. "What's she famous for?"

"Her terrible perfume," Nicholas said in a voice so low that Sam had to strain to hear him.

"It's the scent of rotting flowers. It wafts up your nose until you're fit to choke on it!"

Two strange and unexpected things happened then, at nearly the same time.

A shadow passed over the friends; Sam looked up, just in time to spot a ghostly image float past—or through?—one of the windows in the nearest tower.

Sofia looked a little sick. "I think I can smell—"

Just then, Sam caught a whiff of the dreadful scent too. It was thick and sweet and awful all at once, like the compost bin at the Community Center when he forgot to empty it.

Nicholas's eyes were as wide as a full moon. "It's her!" he breathed. "The Woman in White!"

"I want to see her!" Sofia exclaimed.

Sam hung back just a little.

"Isn't, uh, smelling her enough?" he asked.

"Come on," Sofia urged him. "This might be our one and only chance to see a ghost!"

And, surprising even himself, Sam found himself intrigued.

"Okay," he said, his camera at the ready. "But if we see a ghost, I'm getting proof."

The three set off on a speedy but silent trip through the Tower, trying to follow the dreadful scent. When they reached the upper tower where Sam thought he'd seen something, everyone paused at the threshold.

Did they dare go inside? Sofia looked over at Sam, searching his face for the answer to a question she hadn't asked.

In response, he nodded and held up his camera.

31

Sam was ready for whatever lurked behind the heavy wooden door.

"On the count of three," Nicholas whispered.

Sofia's hand hovered over the doorknob.

"One . . . two . . ."

C-r-r-r-r-e-e-e-e-a-k!

Sam jumped at the shrieking of the rusty hinges. But nothing else moved.

The room at the top of the tower was empty.

Sam lowered his camera. A mixture of relief, disappointment, and a little embarrassment swirled inside him.

"Sorry, everybody," he said with a small shrug. "I really thought I saw . . . Well, anyway, I didn't mean to lead us on a wild-goose chase."

"A wild ghost chase!" Sofia joked. She wandered over to the pointed windows and gazed out at the sky. Just then, Sofia spotted something that made her freeze.

"What is it?" Sam asked.

"If we hurry, we can still solve part of this mystery," Sofia said, her words tumbling out in a rush. "Follow me!"

This time, the three friends didn't worry about stealth. Their feet clambered over the stone steps as they raced back down to the green grass, just in time to discover a woman pushing a wheelbarrow of faded flowers!

"Afternoon, loves," she said, motioning to the blooms. "Pretty, aren't they? Leftover wedding flowers from the chapel. It looks like the happy couple left them behind."

As soon as the woman had moved on, Sam, Sofia, and Nicholas looked at one another and burst into laughter.

5

Birds of Prey

Nicholas walked Sam and Sofia back to the area where they'd first met. Sam couldn't help but worry a little. Had they spent too much time chasing ghosts at the Tower of London? Had they spent too much of the scooter's battery?

"So where should we go next?" Sofia asked.

"I'm not sure," Sam replied. "Nicholas, Sofia needs to learn about falconers. Any suggestions?"

Nicholas didn't hesitate. "That's an easy one!" he replied. "The Falconry Centre in West Midlands. It's amazing to visit and see the birds up close. There are real falconers who work there, and they'll even show you how they fly the birds."

"Really?" Sofia gasped. "We can actually meet the falcons?"

"And owls, and eagles, and vultures," Nicholas continued, ticking each one off on his fingers as Sofia scribbled in her notebook. "There's all manner of birds of prey at the Falconry Centre."

Sam turned to Sofia, his eyebrows raised. "That's definitely our next destination!"

Sofia's eyes were shining with enthusiasm. "We have to make sure we go to King Arthur's Great Halls, though," she said. "With the scooter's battery and all, I don't want you to lose the chance to learn more about knights. And we can't get stranded."

"Stranded?" Nicholas asked. "It can't be all that bad. We're in the middle of London. I can take you to the bus, or the tube, or we can hail a cab."

Sam and Sofia exchanged a glance. "None of those options would get us home," Sam said slowly. "It's a very long trip. I mean, it's short. I mean, it *would* be long, but we know a sort of shortcut."

Now Nicholas looked even more confused.

"Okay," Sofia said. She turned to Nicholas. "I'm about to tell you something that will be pretty impossible to believe. And you're invited to come with us, but first, can you keep a secret?"

"I'll do my best, mate," Nicholas promised.

Sofia and Sam took turns telling Nicholas about the red scooter. Their stories about their adventures around the world left him speechless.

When they reached the shaded spot where they had hidden the red scooter, Nicholas flashed an excited smile. "Brilliant," he said. "I can't wait to see how it works!"

"I'm surprised you believe us," Sofia said.

Nicholas grinned. "I chase ghosts around the Tower all the time," he joked. "Surely a world-traveling scooter is possible. But how exactly does it take you places? That part I just don't understand."

"It's hard to describe," Sam admitted. "It's probably best for you to see for yourself."

The three friends climbed aboard the scooter, with Sam at the controls. When everyone was settled, he gave Nicholas one very important instruction: "Hold on tight!"

"*Vamos!*" Sofia said.

"*Vamos!*" Nicholas repeated.

Whiz . . . Zoom . . . FOOP!

6

Any Volunteers?

Moments later, the red scooter arrived in West Midlands. As soon as the golden sparkles began to fade, Nicholas tumbled off the scooter. "Amazing!" he sputtered. "Incredible! Unbelievable!"

Nicholas took some paces, walking back and forth in front of the scooter, rubbing his eyes. "Way more impressive than a wheelbarrow of flowers," he said.

"You weren't scared, on your very first ride?" Sofia asked.

Nicholas shook his head. "I didn't have time to be scared," he said. "By the time I realized what was happening, we'd already arrived!"

"There it is," Sofia said, gazing at The Falconry Centre, a series of low, wooden buildings nestled among the grassy landscape. What had really captured Sofia's attention, though, were the aviaries: large, enclosed spaces covered with wire and netting so that the birds at The Falconry Centre could fly and experience nature while staying protected.

The trio paused for a moment to listen. Under the whistling of the wind, they could hear something else: clicks and coos and squawks.

It was the birds, chattering to one another.

"I can't wait to see them up close," Sofia said quietly, almost to herself.

"Neither can I!" Nicholas replied. "I haven't been here in ages."

After hiding the red scooter in a nearby grove of trees, the three friends approached the Falconry Centre. The sky was still overcast, but every so often a beam of sunlight pierced through the clouds.

A large tour group had just arrived. Sam, Sofia, and Nicholas stayed near the edge of the crowd as they all walked through the entrance.

"Must be a school trip," Nicholas said, motioning to the matching clothes worn by the kids in the group. "Almost every student in England wears a uniform to school."

Sam could tell Sofia was only partially listening as she gazed at the aviaries filled with enormous birds. She held up her notebook in anticipation. "Come on!" she exclaimed. "Let's spot some birds!"

"Ready!" Sam replied, holding up his camera.

With over 80 birds living in the Falconry Centre's aviaries, Sam knew Sofia would have to move fast to see as many as possible—but she always lingered at her favorites, like the snowy owl, the yellow-eyed sparrowhawk, and the golden eagle. Sam, hovering just behind her, made sure to snap lots of photos.

Click-click!

He had a feeling Sofia would be delighted to see them after they got back to Compass Court.

When they reached the falcons, Sofia stopped and stared. "They're so beautiful," she breathed. "Can you imagine how they must soar through the sky, navigating wind currents we can't even see?"

"I don't think we'll have to imagine it," Nicholas replied. He pointed to a sign. "There's going to be a flight demonstration starting in just a few minutes!"

The only thing that could tear Sofia away from the aviaries was the promise of watching the falcons, eagles, and hawks in flight. The pals hurried over to the demonstration area so that they could find spots right in front. It overlooked a grassy hillside dotted with trees that led to a forest.

The crowd slowly swelled behind them, and after several minutes, a woman appeared. She was wearing an olive-green shirt over heavy canvas pants, with a tough leather glove that stretched all the way above her elbow. But what really stood out was the enormous bird perched on the woman's arm.

The bird shifted on its taloned feet and turned its head to stare at the crowd with a bright, beady eye.

"Good afternoon!" she announced. "My name is Catherine, and I'm one of the falconers here at the Falconry Centre."

"I can't believe it. She's a real, live falconer!" Sofia

whispered in amazement.

"And this is Ridley, one of our majestic white-tailed eagles. He'll help me lead today's flying display," Catherine continued.

Under ordinary circumstances, Sam would have clapped and cheered, but he wasn't sure if sudden noise or motion would startle Ridley, so he stayed very still. The entire audience sat mesmerized.

"Falconry is an ancient sport," Catherine told the group. "Historians believe it dates back to ancient Mongolia, or possibly the Middle East, before becoming popular in Europe. Of course, it wasn't just a sport." She lifted her arm and walked the bird in front of the guests. "Falconry was also an important method of hunting, as the birds were used to catch quarry, or prey. For falconers, that meant meat to feed their families."

Sam couldn't decide which he liked better: watching the falcon or watching Sofia watch the falcon. Her eyes never left Ridley during Catherine's demonstration, and her hand never stopped writing notes in her special notebook. Sam saw her write off the page more than once as she stared transfixed at Catherine and Ridley.

"These birds glide through the air, scouting prey from great heights, then swoop down and attack with deadly accuracy to catch their prey," Catherine explained.

The crowd gasped in awe as Ridley soared off Catherine's gloved arm, caught a clump of quail feathers tossed in the air by an assistant, and then returned to perch on Catherine's arm in one seamless flight.

Catherine smiled at the crowd. "I see we've got some young bird lovers with us today. Any volunteers to fly one of our owls?"

Sofia's hand shot in the air before Catherine had finished the sentence. Nicholas's hand followed quickly behind.

"Oh good!" Catherine said, smiling broadly. "Two volunteers is just what we need."

The assistant hurried over with long leather gloves for Sofia and Nicholas. Sam raised his camera as he watched his friends slide their hands into the gloves.

Click-click!

"Now, to be a falconer, you have to be strong,"

Catherine told them. "Some of our birds weigh well over half a stone."

"Like, a big stone? A small one?" Sam asked.

Catherine laughed kindly. "For our American visitors," she said, "a stone is how we measure weight. One stone is equal to about 14 pounds.

We have birds that weigh a solid, ahh, ten pounds or so."

"Balancing ten pounds on your arm?" Sofia said, stretching out her left arm. "Got it."

"You also have to be brave," Catherine continued. "Raptors, or birds of prey, are ferocious hunters, and you're inviting them to perch on your body."

"Oh, Sofia is definitely brave," Sam spoke up with a grin. "And Nicholas too. We just watched him hunt a ghost!"

The crowd murmured, impressed, as Nicholas beamed with pride.

"Looks like I chose a great set of volunteers," Catherine said. "Most of all, though," she continued, lowering her voice, "You have to be calm. The birds are highly sensitive. They can sometimes pick up on our feelings and emotions. If you're skittish and nervous, they'll be able to tell, and odds are they'll start feeling skittish and nervous too."

"Calm. Brave. Strong," Sofia repeated, ticking each one off on her fingers.

"Do you feel ready?" Catherine asked.

Sofia took a deep breath. "Ready!" she replied.

"Ready!" Nicholas said.

"Wonderful," Catherine replied. "Just hold your gloved arm out as straight as you can. Yes, you've got it! Now, bring out Jester!"

When the assistant returned, she had a beautiful owl perched on her arm. He watched the crowd with wide, wondering eyes that peeked out from his silky feathers. When he spotted Sofia, he seemed to recognize the position of her arm, straight and steady.

In a blink—in a blur—the small owl fluttered over and perched soundly on Sofia's arm! Sam could tell she was holding her breath, and after a moment, Sam realized he was holding his breath too.

"Oh, well done, Jester! And Sofia!" Catherine said. Then, smiling, she added. "Jester can be a bit of a mischief-maker. Sometimes he flies right past the arm to land on the head!"

Sofia swallowed back her giggles, but the smile on her face was wider than ever.

"All right, Nicholas, was it?" Catherine said. "Walk about ten big steps that way . . . yes, that's right! Now go ahead and hold your arm out, and we'll see if Jester still feels like following the rules."

Sofia and Nicholas locked eyes, standing like mirror images of each other with their arms outstretched and a gulf of ten feet between them.

Then, without warning, Jester took off! He zipped straight over to Nicholas's arm, where he perched for a few moments before making an unexpected return trip to Sofia. Sam grinned even bigger as he watched Sofia think—and act—fast. She raised her arm and held it steady just in time for Jester to grasp onto her glove with his curved talons. Sofia didn't have to say a word for Sam to know that it was one of the best moments of her life.

Jester, however, had plenty to say! A series of chirping coos seemed to echo from deep within his throat.

Then Jester shook his wings and lost a feather! The breeze twirled it through the air, carrying it toward the watching crowd.

Sam didn't hesitate. He leaped forward and caught the feather just before it blew out of reach.

From his perch on Sofia's arm, Jester bobbed his head. It almost looked like he was nodding his approval.

"Looks like you've made a new friend, Jester!" Catherine said, still smiling.

"Friends for life!" Sofia added.

"Perhaps you'd like a turn with Ridley?"

Catherine offered. "He's probably ready for a good fly, but he might perch for another moment or two."

"Oh, please?" Sofia replied.

The assistant whisked Jester away as Catherine approached. From his perch on Catherine's arm, Ridley eyed Sofia curiously. Sofia held out her arm, as straight and steady as she could.

The transfer was seamless. Ridley moved one talon, then the next, and soon he was perched on Sofia's arm! Sofia held her breath as she stood, motionless, doing everything in her power to prolong the moment.

"He's incredible," Sofia whispered.

Ridley blinked—or winked—and bobbed his head as if he appreciated the compliment. Then he stretched out his wings, leaped into the air, and soared away.

7
A Difficult Decision

When the flying demonstration was over, Sam, Sofia, and Nicholas stopped by the café for a quick snack.

"You have to try some scones with jam," Nicholas said, pointing to small, golden treats that looked like a cross between a biscuit and an unfrosted cake. "Oh, and we can get some sandwiches, too! Egg and cress, or perhaps cheese and pickle . . ."

"Cheese and pickle? That sounds good!" Sam said.

The sandwich turned out to be delicious, with thick slices of crumbly Cheddar cheese and a sweet-spicy vegetable relish that wasn't exactly what Sam expected when Nicholas said "pickle." He loved every bite!

"Thank you for telling us about the Falconry Centre," Sofia told Nicholas as they walked back to the scooter. "You were right. It was an incredible place to visit!"

Then she turned to Sam. "And thank you for encouraging us to come here. I can't wait to be a falconer at the Faire!"

"You'll be the best falconer the Faire could ever have!" Sam replied. "Now let's get back to the scooter. We can drop Nicholas back at the Tower of London and then zip back to Compass Court before the battery is completely out of power."

"Actually . . ." Sofia began.

That's when Sam noticed it: that familiar twinkle sparkling in her eyes.

"Our trip isn't over," Sofia continued. "Tintagel beckons!" She pressed the button on the red scooter to turn it on.

But Sam shook his head. "Nope. No way. Not this trip," he said firmly. "Look at the battery light. It's at 23 percent! I mean, it's not even green anymore. It's yellow!"

"Yellow doesn't mean stop," Sofia said.

"But it means slow down! I'm sure there are books about knights in the library at Compass Community Center. I can do more research when we get home."

"We can do it, Sam, I know we can!" Sofia

urged him. "I've been keeping track of how quickly the scooter is losing power, and it's at a constant rate. We have time."

"Losing power at a constant rate? You're sounding like Aunt Charlie," Sam joked.

Sofia, however, looked completely serious. She showed Sam a page in her notebook that was covered with numbers. "If we go to Tintagel and stay for less than

70% - 25% = 45% used

45% battery used = 88 minutes passed

About half that amount remaining . . .

88 minutes/2 = about 44 minutes left!!

an hour—maybe forty-five minutes, just to be safe—we should have just enough power to get Nicholas back to the Tower of London and then return to Compass Court."

Sam looked down at the page, then up, then down again. "When did you do all these calculations?" he asked in surprise.

Sofia shrugged. "I'm a fast writer, " she said.

Sam shook his head again. "But what if

something unexpected happens and we get stuck?"

There was a pause before Sofia spoke again. "You know who would take the risk? A knight," she finally said.

Her words were full of kindness and encouragement, and Sam felt them ignite something inside of him. If he was going to be a knight, he'd have to be brave.

"You're right," Sam said. He grinned at his friends. "It's why we came all this way. Let's do it

before we lose any more time!"

Then Sam turned to Nicholas. "You should get a say," Sam told him. "We can drop you off before we go to Tintagel, if you want. Just in case the battery doesn't last as long as we expect."

"And miss the rest of the adventure?" Nicholas exclaimed. "No way, mate! I'm with you to the end."

"Then *vamos!*" Sofia declared.

Everybody scrambled onto the scooter. Before the scooter had even finished asking where they wanted to go, Sam had typed in the answer.

Whiz . . . Zoom . . . FOOP!

8

Tintagel

The golden sparkles had barely begun to fade when Sam leaped off the red scooter, his heart hammering in his chest. At last, he was about to go straight to the source and learn how King Arthur's daring knights had once lived!

Sofia checked her watch. "I'll keep track of the time," she announced, "so we don't stay too long. *Vamos, vamos, vamos!*"

It was easy to find King Arthur's Great Halls; there were plenty of signs to lead the way, and plenty of visitors heading in that direction.

Whatever Sam had imagined on the trip to King Arthur's Great Halls, he never could have been prepared for the reality of seeing it with his own eyes. It was not some ancient castle rising from mist-cloaked cliffs like he'd imagined. Instead, Sam found himself gazing up at a grand stone building that looked more like a mansion than a castle.

Sam wandered a bit away from the others and grabbed a brochure at the ticket stand. "This definitely seems like the right place to learn about knights," he told his friends as he skimmed the brochure.

Then Sam read something that stunned him so much he was speechless for a moment. He read it again to make sure he hadn't misunderstood.

"King Arthur's Great Halls was built in the 1930s. That's hundreds of years after King Arthur's time!" he said, pointing at different pictures in the brochure. "That's not his throne. That's not the real Round Table. It's all just a . . . replication."

"So it's more like a theme park," Sofia said slowly. "But without the rides."

"It's like a—a—a reenactment," Sam said. "They've done their best to imagine what it would've been like, for people today to experience."

"Exactly like we're doing with the Faire!" Sofia exclaimed. "I'm sure we can learn lots about King Arthur here." She pointed at the brochure. "See, they're having demonstrations and classes today, and—ooh, what's that? The Knight Show? Sounds promising!"

"Definitely," Sam replied. "But it doesn't start for a while. I don't know if we have enough time—"

"Leave that to me," Sofia reminded him, tapping her watch.

Just then, Sam noticed another sign.

He didn't know why it caught his attention or why it seemed so important. All Sam knew, really, was that he wanted to follow the winding path to Tintagel Castle and see it for himself.

"Should we check it out?" Sam asked the others. "Before the Knight Show begins, I mean?"

"Why not?" Nicholas replied. "I've never been to Tintagel Castle before."

To reach Tintagel Castle, the friends first had to cross a long bridge over a dizzying chasm. On the other side, high on the cliffs above the choppy sea, Sam, Sofia, and Nicholas discovered the ruins of Tintagel Castle. It was nowhere near as well preserved as the Tower of London. The weathered stones hinted at the greatness that had once existed there, a fortress overlooking the vast ocean below.

"Legend says that Tintagel Castle may have been the birthplace of King Arthur," Sofia read from a sign. "Historical records show that many great rulers from ancient times inhabited this space, which was strengthened by natural defenses like the steep cliffs, the rough seas, and the rocky landscape."

Sofia paused and looked up with wide eyes. "That's the truth," she said. "Can you imagine how frightening it would be to climb these cliffs in a rainstorm?"

"No thanks!" Nicholas said, laughing.

Sofia read a little more. "When conditions are safe, visitors can climb down to the beach and peer into the depths of Merlin's Cave."

"We'll definitely have to come back some day,"

Sam declared, "to see Merlin's Cave."

"Sam! Sofia! Check it out!" Nicholas called.

They hurried over to join him in an area of wild grasses and weeds that seemed organized into squares and rectangles, split into sections by carefully arranged rocks.

"This was a medieval settlement," Nicholas explained. "The buildings are gone now, but the foundations remain."

"Wow," Sofia said in wonder. She found a long rectangle made of rocks and stood in the middle with her hands on her hips. "Maybe this was the aviary," she said. "Maybe if I were a falconer back then, I would have taken care of all the birds here."

Sam took some careful steps around the ruins.

"Maybe this was the Great Hall of the castle," he said. "Maybe if I were a knight, I would have come here every day to serve the king."

"Maybe you would've *been* the king!" Sofia exclaimed. "All hail King Sam!"

Just then, the sound of trumpets echoed across the ruins. The three friends froze, staring at one another with wide eyes.

"They're hailing King Sam!" Sofia whispered as the trumpets blared again.

"No!" Sam exclaimed. "The Knight Show—it's about to begin!"

9

Center Stage

As fast as they dared, the three friends crossed through the rocky ruins, over the swaying bridge, and back to the path. Not far from King Arthur's Great Halls, they found an outdoor stage surrounded by a crowd.

The man standing center stage was wearing a full suit of armor that clinked and clanked when he moved. His costume gleamed under the bright beams of sunshine that broke through the clouds.

"Welcome, welcome to the Knight Show!" he announced in a booming voice. "I'm Sir David, and it's my solemn duty to teach you the finer points of becoming a knight."

He paused as he slowly scanned the crowd, a serious expression on his face. "And a more worthy class of pupils I've not yet seen!" Sir David declared.

Then—**clang!**

The metal visor on his helmet fell with a thunderous twang, making everyone laugh, even Sir David himself.

"Most people remember knights as brave warriors," Sir David continued, his voice muffled behind the heavy visor. "The legends of King Arthur, though, tell us that they were more than just fighters. King Arthur wanted all his knights to be equal. That's why he seated them at a round table, instead of one shaped like a rectangle where knights might compete to sit at the head of the table."

Sam stood a little straighter. If he were a knight, he'd want to sit at a round table too.

Sir David lifted his visor and looked out into the crowd. "Even so, not just anyone could become a knight," he said. "And there was no one path to do so. If a soldier did something exceptionally brave in battle—well, he might be knighted on the spot, right there on the battlefield, in recognition of his daring courage. And that was the easy way."

"The easy way?" Sofia whispered beside Sam.

"The other way took a lot more time and effort," he continued. "Now, if I could get some volunteers."

Sam felt a little push on his shoulder.

It was Sofia, nudging him forward.

"Sam!" she whispered. "Go! Volunteer!"

He shook his head. "No, I'll just watch."

Sam felt another push. Nicholas was urging him forward, too!

"You already have the best parts of a knight inside you," Sofia said softly. "You were brave searching the Tower of London for ghosts. Then you made sure we went to the Falconry Centre for me, instead of putting yourself first. And you're agile. You snatched Jester's feather right out of the air. I watched you do it."

Sam ducked his head, a little embarrassed. Was Sofia right? Was he more like a knight than he knew?

All the kids in the audience waved their hands wildly, hoping that Sir David would pick them.

Suddenly, Sam raised his hand too, as high as he could!

"You, you, you . . ." Sir David said, pointing into the crowd. "And you."

Was Sir David's shiny silver finger really pointing at Sam?

It was!

Sofia and Nicholas cheered as they pushed Sam—who was still a little shocked that he'd been chosen—toward the stage. He climbed up with the other kids who had volunteered, but not before Sofia grabbed his camera.

"I'll be the photographer this time," she said.

The rough boards of the stage creaked as Sam walked over to Sir David.

"Let's see," Sir David said, eyeing his volunteers. "You two will be our pages, and you two will be our squires."

Sam found himself sorted into the squire group and took a step to the right. He glanced out of the corner of his eye at Sofia, who was watching in astonishment.

"Now, while most knights came into the knighthood through family connections, there were some other paths," Sir David said. "Around age seven, a young boy who had his sights set on achieving knighthood could be apprenticed to a knight. He would live in the knight's house and be the knight's servant. He was called a page."

Age seven? Sam thought in surprise. *That's so young to leave your family and start training!*

Sam watched with interest as Sir David demonstrated the different chores a page might do, from serving food at mealtimes to learning how to ride a horse. Pages even got to practice fighting with pretend weapons!

Then—at last—Sir David approached Sam and the squire group.

"After several years, a hardworking page could become a squire, usually around age fourteen," Sir David explained. "The training grew even more intense as squires got older.

They were expected to be skilled at horseback riding, especially guiding the horse with just their knees and feet, since their hands would be holding a shield and a lance. That's this long pole with the sharp, pointy bit at the end. You certainly wouldn't want to meet one of these on the battlefield, I should say!"

Sam watched in amazement as Sir David unveiled a display of wooden swords.

"Knights' weapons were all too real, but these are stage weapons, and safe to use," Sir David said. "Still, treat them as if they were real."

Sam intended to. If he pretended the weapons were real, it might make him feel more like a genuine knight. When Sir David unexpectedly tossed a sword in Sam's direction, Sam caught it without hesitating for even a moment!

Everyone cheered, and when Sam heard the **click-click** of his camera, he knew that Sofia was taking tons of pictures.

"And now, for the armor!" Sir David announced. His eyes scanned the group on stage before resting on Sam. "You, there. Step forward, if you please."

"Me?" Sam asked.

"As you'll soon see," Sir David said, "it was no easy task for a knight to dress in a full suit of armor. Let's demonstrate! These overlapping strips of metal were called *lames*. They made it easier for knights to move."

Sam stood very still as a stagehand fitted the suit of armor around him.

"We won't put on the full suit. That would be way too heavy for a lad your size," Sir David said.

Even so, Sam was astonished by the weight of the vest, arm plates, and helmet (which was called a *helm*).

"How did they manage to fight battles wearing all this stuff?" he asked, his voice echoing back to him under the helmet.

"It was slow going," Sir David answered. "Knights had to be very strong, but you can imagine how slowly they moved, encumbered by all this extra weight. It was a tall order."

Sam watched from inside his helm as Sir David continued. "Being a knight meant more than just excellence in battle and mastery of swordsmanship," he said. "Knights were expected to uphold the code of chivalry—to leave the violence on the battlefield and protect anyone in need. And if someone proved themself worthy, their courage and character would be rewarded." Sir David flashed a smile. "Now, if my esteemed volunteers would please kneel."

Sam's heart started pounding again as he lowered himself to his knees. Sir David pulled a sword from his belt. This one wasn't wooden; it was large and shiny, with a handle encrusted with glittering gems. Sir David walked slowly and deliberately over to Sam.

"What's your name, lad?" he said in a strong,

low voice.

"S-Sam. It's Sam."

Sir David turned back to the breathless crowd. "The ceremony by which an individual was knighted," he said, "was called an *accolade*. It had several components, but dubbing was the most important."

Sir David took a deep breath, and his voice rang out with even greater clarity. "Sam," he announced. "I dub thee Sir Knight."

Sam didn't move a muscle as the flat side of the glittering sword gently tapped his right shoulder—**ting!**—and then his left—**ting!**

The sound of metal on metal reverberated across the wooden stage, then over the heads of the watching crowd.

One moment later, Sofia called, "Sir Sam!" in such a gleeful and joyous voice that Sir David broke out in a cheerful laugh.

"Sir Sam!" echoed the others.

Sam gazed through the opening in the helmet and tried to memorize everything about the incredible moment.

He already knew, though, that the weight of the armor and the feel of the sword tapping his shoulders was something he'd never forget.

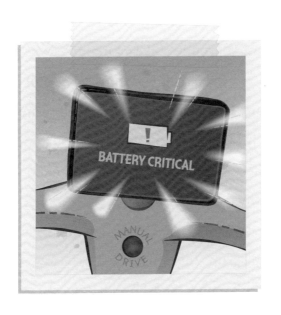

10
Battery Critical

After the Knight Show, Sofia and Nicholas crowded around Sam, wanting him to relive every detail of his time on the stage. Sofia was eager to show him all the photos she'd taken too. She'd captured every moment!

"Do you feel different, mate?" Nicholas asked. "I mean, do you feel like a knight?"

"I . . . I think I do?" Sam replied, still a little embarrassed by all the attention. "It seemed like a really big deal up on the stage, you know?"

"That's because it was a big deal!" Sofia exclaimed.

"Mostly, I feel like I understand it all so much better," Sam told his friends. "How people became knights, and how they were supposed to treat others."

"You'll be a great knight at the Faire," Sofia said. "Sir Sam!"

"I hope so," Sam replied. "But you know what we haven't done yet?"

"What?" Sofia asked.

Sam held up his camera. "Selfie time!"

"I could take your picture," Nicholas volunteered.

"No! You've got to be in it!" Sofia replied,

beckoning him over. The three friends perched on the edge of the stage. "Everyone say . . . cheese-and-pickle sandwich!"

"Cheese-and-pickle sandwich!" the three friends said, all at the same time.

Click-click!

"Got it!" Sam announced. He turned to Nicholas. "I'll send you one after we get home."

Home.

Sam suddenly remembered the scooter's battery. He'd lost complete track of time during the Knight Show. "The scooter—" he began.

Sofia seemed to read his thoughts. "We should still be okay," she replied. "But we need to go. *Now.*"

Without another word, the three friends raced back to the red scooter. Breathless, they climbed aboard. Sam hit the power button and waited.

Nothing happened.

Uh-oh, he thought nervously. His finger pushed the button again. This time, the screen lit up, but not how it usually did.

"Sofia," Sam said, "how are we going to get home?"

11

A Hard Reset

"We . . . it should . . . here, let me try," Sofia said.

Sam slid back from the controls to make room for her.

"I sure wish Aunt Charlie had included an

91

instruction manual!" Sofia said, sounding worried. "Wait! Remember when Papai's phone was acting funny? And he did a . . . a hard reset?

"Do you think it would work on the scooter?" Sam asked.

"It's worth a shot," Sofia said. "But do you know how to do one on the scooter?"

"I saw Aunt Charlie reboot it once," Sam said. He tapped the screen, then pushed the button and held it down.

The screen went black.

The seconds ticked away.

"Now what?" Sam asked urgently.

"We count," Sofia said. "Fifty-seven, fifty-eight, fifty-nine, sixty!"

She pushed the button again and, to everyone's relief, the scooter's main screen appeared. It was barely visible, though, its light more dim than usual, and a blinking banner at the top declared "LOW POWER! SAFE MODE."

"I knew you two could do it!" Nicholas said.

Then everything happened very fast.

"Tower of London," Sofia whispered as her fingers tapped on the touchscreen.

"Hold on!" Sam shouted.

Whiz . . . Zoom . . . FOOP!

In a swirling flash, they returned to the Tower of London, where they said a hasty goodbye to Nicholas as he hopped off the red scooter. He waved wildly at them from the grassy lawn, the ravens fluttering behind him.

Sam and Sofia scarcely had the chance to wave back before they were surrounded, once more, by the familiar sparkling dome of light.

Whiz . . . Zoom . . . FOOP!

And just like that, Sam and Sofia found themselves back in Aunt Charlie's lab. Sam's head was spinning. Everything was just as they'd left it . . . but the scooter's screen was black. They had used the very last burst of power to get home.

"We made it!" Sam exclaimed as he jumped off the scooter. "I can't believe it!"

"You know what? Neither can I!" Sofia admitted. "That was close. Really close!"

"Maybe too close," Sam said, his eyes wide. "From now on, I'll always double-check to make sure the scooter is plugged in before I go to bed at night."

"Good idea," Sofia said. "I always love our adventures, but you know what? Coming home is one of my favorite parts."

"Mine too," Sam agreed. "And we have to get ready for the Faire! It's got to be starting soon!"

"That's right!" Sofia remembered. "Meet you at the jousting arena?"

"You got it," Sam replied. "Just don't forget your falcon!"

12

Past and Present

ater that day, a feeling of merriment filled the air as Sam walked toward Compass Community Center. Sam could hear the chatter of voices and the cheerful melody of lutes and fiddles. And of course, there was laughter.

Thankfully, Sam's costume armor was not nearly as heavy or clunky as the set he'd tried on at the Knight Show. He'd cut strips of cardboard and covered them with foil, then overlapped the strips into a suit of armor that was just his size. He couldn't wait to show everybody!

Sam wasn't the only one hurrying toward the Faire in a state of excitement. Sofia was half a block away, waving wildly.

"Hey!" Sam called. "How'd you recognize me?"

"You're pretty shiny in the sunshine!" Sofia replied. "What an impressive suit of armor, Sir Sam!"

"Thanks," Sam said. "And that's a pretty incredible falconer costume you made!"

Sofia was wearing a long shirt that belonged to Mama Lyla. It fit just like an old-fashioned tunic. On Sofia's left hand was one of Papai Luiz's sturdy work gloves. She grinned as she thrust out her arm as if she were still at the

Falconry Centre. The best part was that Sofia had attached one of her stuffed animals, a bird she had named Beatrix, to her left arm.

"What kind of falconer would I be if I didn't bring my bird everywhere I go to get her used to being around people?" she joked. "Beatrix is very well behaved. She won't peck at any of the Faire visitors."

Sam was laughing too, as they entered the Faire. Aunt Charlie and Mama Lyla were standing at the entrance, an archway covered with boughs of greenery and fresh wildflowers. Even Bertram the donkey looked especially festive, with a wreath of flowers around his neck that he kept trying to nibble!

"What do we have here?" Aunt Charlie exclaimed when she spotted Sam and Sofia.

"Tell us about your roles at the Faire."

"I'm a falconer!" Sofia said proudly.

"Tell me more!" Aunt Charlie said.

"Well, the role changed over time but it was important in many ways," Sofia said. "Falconers helped families have enough food to eat. They were part of a popular sport that people loved. But mostly they learned how to care for these incredible birds. That's my favorite part."

"Wonderful!" Mama Lyla said. Then she turned to Sam. "What say you, Sir Sam?"

Sam thought carefully before he answered.

"I wasn't sure if being a knight was right for me," he began. "But the things that King Arthur and the Knights of the Round Table stood for, like fairness and justice and equality, well, those matter just as much today. If I can bring a little bit of that to the Faire, I'll do it proudly."

"A noble pursuit, to be sure," Mama Lyla said. "I see you've both done your research."

"Perhaps with the help of something in my lab," Aunt Charlie said.

Sam gulped. *Did Aunt Charlie know they'd taken the scooter?* Before he could wonder any further, Aunt Charlie gave him a wink as Papai Luiz pointed across the Faire.

"You two might want to hurry," he said. "There's always a crowd at the maypole dance, and I'm sure they'd love a visit from a falconer and a knight."

"A maypole dance?" Sam asked. "Never heard of it."

"I guess we still have a lot to learn about medieval times," Sofia said.

"Let's check it out," Sam said.

As they strolled over to the maypole, where bright ribbons fluttered in the breeze, Sam thought of all the places they'd seen and the ways in which the past and the present could combine.

Learning from history isn't just to know about things that happened a long time ago, he thought. *It's a way to use the past to make the future better.*

And Sam had a feeling that King Arthur would agree.

THE END

British Slang Terms & Phrases

- **Ace** - Awesome   - **Any road** - Anyway

- **Bee's Knees** - Excellent   - **Biscuit** - Cookie

- **Brill** - Cool or excellent; short for "brilliant"

- **Car park** - Parking lot

- **Cheerio** - Goodbye

- **Chips** - French fries   - **Cuppa** - Cup of tea

- **Easy peasy** - Easy to do or understand

- **Fortnight** - Two weeks

- **Give us a bell** - Call me on the phone

- **Gobsmacked** - Shocked or surprised

- **Jammy** - Lucky   - **Kip** - Sleep

- **Ledge** - amazing person; short for "legend"

- **Lift** - Elevator   - **Mate** - Friend

- **Nosh** - Food

- **Over the moon** - Overjoyed

- **Porkie** - Lie   - **Proper** - Very or extremely

- **Queue** - Line; to stand in line

- **Rubbish** - Nonsense

- **Ta** - Thank you

- **Trainers** - Tennis shoes; sneakers

- **Trolley** - Shopping cart

- **Uncle Ned** - Bed

- **Wicked** - Great or fabulous

Portuguese Term

- **Vamos!** - Let's go!

Sam and Sofia's Snippets

England is the largest country in Great Britain and the United Kingdom (the UK). It is ruled by a parliamentary democracy under a constitutional monarchy. Monarchy is the oldest form of government in the UK.

Queen Elizabeth II is the longest-reigning monarch to ever serve the United Kingdom of Great Britain and Northern Ireland.

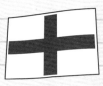 ← The English flag

More tea is enjoyed in the UK than most other countries in the world. Only the Turkish and the Irish drink more tea than the British. Customarily served with a splash of milk and some biscuits (cookies) on the side, there are few things more English than a spot of tea.

Tintagel is a village and parish located in Cornwall, England. The village is a popular place to visit in Great Britain thanks to nearby Tintagel Castle's connections to the legend of King Arthur.

According to a mythical history penned hundreds of years ago by writer Geoffrey of Monmouth, the famed King Arthur was born in Tintagel Castle and grew up to become a legendary warrior.

Many writers have since imagined the various adventures of King Arthur, his mother Igraine, his adviser Merlin, and the Knights of the Round Table. Most stories include references of Tintagel, where the fable of Arthur began.

The Tower of London is a medieval castle that, over the years, has served as a royal residence, a protective fortress, an exotic zoo, and more!

The first record of animals being kept at the Tower dates back to the 1200s, during the reign of King John (1199-1216). Back then, you could find many animals on the castle grounds, from lions and kangaroos to elephants, polar bears, and ostriches.

The Tower's Menagerie was closed in 1835, with the animals safely transported to the London Zoo.

A path called the Wall Walk wraps along the top of the Tower's massive outer wall. From this height, you can *see* the now-famous ravens soaring across the wide lawns.

No one knows exactly when or why the mysterious birds first arrived, but legend has it, if any of the original birds ever leave the Tower, the kingdom will fall. Don't scare them away!

Over the centuries, falconry became an exclusive pastime of British nobility. The strict classes that separated people of different means applied to birds as well. For example, only the king could fly a gyrfalcon, which was considered a rare and noble species. Over time, the social lines faded until, finally, falconry became a sport welcome to everyone.

British Scone Recipe

Ingredients:

- [ ] 1 3/4 cup flour
- [ ] 4 tsp. baking powder
- [ ] 1/3 cup sugar
- [ ] 5 Tbsp. cold butter
- [ ] 2/3 cup cold milk

Scones have been a popular baked good throughout England and the rest of the United Kingdom for more than 500 years. They taste best served warm and are often served with a spot of tea. Best of all, they're fast to make, so you can enjoy scones in no time!

Try this!

Sprinkle cinnamon sugar on top before baking.

Add ½ cup of dried currants to the dough between Steps 3 and 4. (A currant is a type of berry that looks like a tiny raisin when dried.)

Instructions:

1. Preheat the oven to 400 degrees Fahrenheit. Line a baking tray with parchment paper or foil. Set the tray aside.

2. In a large bowl, whisk the flour, baking powder, and sugar together.

3. Cut the butter into small cubes and add it to the flour mixture. Stir and press the butter into the mixture until crumbs the size of small peas are formed. You can use a pastry cutter, two forks, or your hands!

4. Add the milk and stir until just after the dough comes together. It should be pretty sticky.

5. On a floured surface, pat the dough into a disk about ¾-inch thick. Cut the dough into circles with a cookie cutter. Transfer the circles to the tray.

6. Bake for 15-17 minutes, or until the scones are golden brown on top and light brown on the bottom.

7. Serve your scones with jam and butter and a nice cup of tea!

Read through all the recipe instructions with an adult and ask their permission to do this activity. Be sure to ask an adult to do or help with the steps that require an oven.